For Kafka – C.J.

First published 2008 by Walker Books Ltd
87 Vauxhall Walk, London SE11 5HJ

10 9 8 7 6 5 4 3 2 1

This book has been typeset in BodonAntT

Printed in China

British Library Cataloguing in
Publication Data: a catalogue record for
this book is available from
the British Library

ISBN 978-1-84428-156-5

www.walkerbooks.co.uk

Arabella Miller's Tiny Caterpillar

Clare Jarrett

WALKER BOOKS
AND SUBSIDIARIES
LONDON · BOSTON · SYDNEY · AUCKLAND

Little Arabella Miller

met a tiny caterpillar.

One day when she was climbing trees,

she found him crawling on her sleeve.

She said, "Hello, Caterpillar,

my name's Arabella Miller."

Little Arabella Miller

carried stripy Caterpillar

down the garden with great care

and settled in her favourite chair.

She said, "Tiny caterpillar's

safe with Arabella Miller."

Little Arabella Miller
loved her wiggly caterpillar.
First he climbed upon her mother
then upon her baby brother.
Mum said, "Arabella Miller,
put away your caterpillar."

Little Arabella Miller
made a home for Caterpillar.
She stuffed a shoebox full of flowers,
then leaves and grass. It took her hours.
She said, "Tiny caterpillar,
stay with Arabella Miller."

Little Arabella Miller
gathered food for Caterpillar.
Curly cabbage, crisp and crunchy,
frizzy parsley, fresh and munchy.
He mixed his meals up: first came brunch,
then dinner, breakfast, tea and lunch.

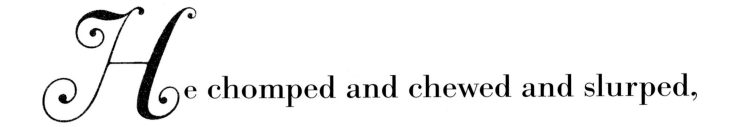

He chomped and chewed and slurped,

then CRACK!

His skin split all along his back.

And underneath it, big and baggy,

was a new one, soft and saggy.

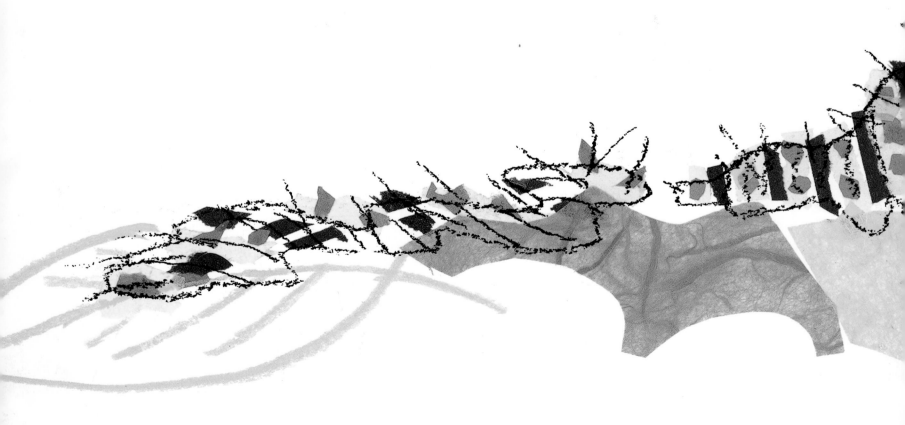

He ate and ate and grew and grew,

for that's what caterpillars do.

On sunny days and in the rain,

he shed his skin time and again.

One hazy, lazy afternoon

she watched him work and hummed a tune.

He made a shell with him inside –

the perfect, cosy place to hide.

Weeks went by and Arabella
missed her friendly caterpillar.
She pictured him curled up in bed
inside his house upon its thread.
Every day she saw it gleaming,
wondered what he could
be dreaming.

*T*hen one day her caterpillar
puzzled Arabella Miller.

She saw him moving, poking through,
and out he came, completely new.

"Oh!" said Arabella Miller.

"You're so different, Caterpillar."

She held her breath and watched in awe
as he was changing more and more.
Bright wings unfolded, stretched to dry,
then up he floated to the sky.

"Goodbye, goodbye, away you fly,
my very special butterfly!"

The Life-cycle of a Butterfly

The Egg

The female butterfly finds a plant and lays her eggs, often on the underside of the leaves. She chooses a type of plant that her baby caterpillars will like to eat when they hatch. It takes two to three weeks for the caterpillars to develop inside the eggs.

The Caterpillar

When a caterpillar is ready to hatch, it eats a hole through the shell of the egg and wriggles out. The caterpillar's main purpose is to grow. It does this by eating constantly, shedding its skin each time it becomes too tight. The new skin underneath is larger, with room for growth. The caterpillar will take one to two months to become fully grown.

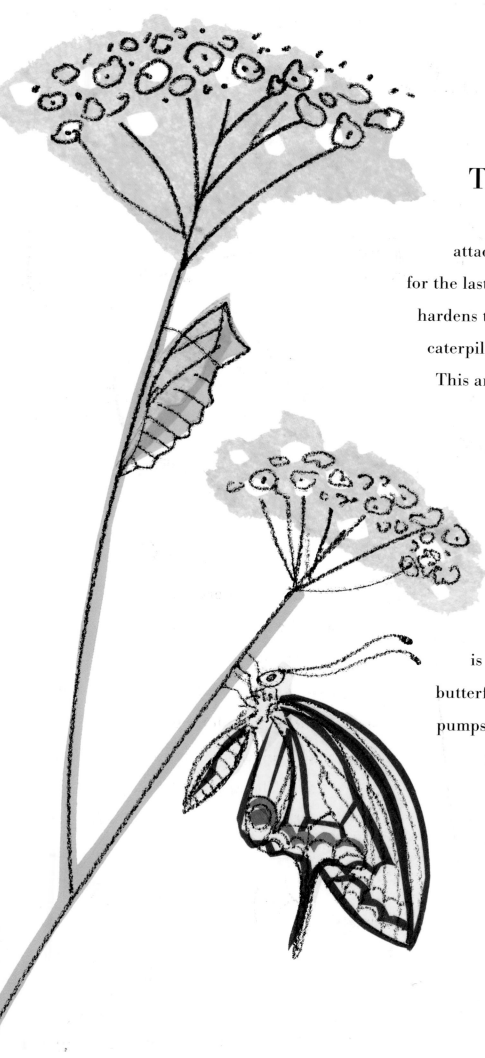

The Chrysalis (or Pupa)

The caterpillar spins a length of silk, attaches itself to a plant, then sheds its skin for the last time. Underneath is a chrysalis, which hardens to become a protective shell. Inside, the caterpillar begins to transform into a butterfly. This amazing change is called metamorphosis and takes about two weeks.

The Butterfly

The chrysalis becomes transparent and breaks apart when the butterfly is ready to hatch. When it crawls out, the butterfly's wings are wet and crumpled, but it pumps blood into them until they reach their full size. It dries its wings in the sun to make them strong. Now it is ready to fly off and find a mate.

In time, the butterfly will lay its own eggs and the life-cycle will begin again.